dauid orme

has written too many books to count, ranging from poetry to non-fiction.

When he is not writing he travels around the UK, giving performances and running writing workshops.

David is a huge science fiction fan and has the biggest collection of science fiction magazines that the Starchasers have ever seen.

starchasers

the lost explorers

by

dauid orme

illustrated by
jorge mongiouoi

Ransom

starchasers

The Lost Explorers
by David Orme

Illustrated by Jorge Mongiovi

Published by Ransom Publishing Ltd.
51 Southgate Street, Winchester, Hants. SO23 9EH, UK

www.ransom.co.uk

ISBN 978 184167 763 7

First published in 2009

A CIP catalogue record of this book is available from the British Library.

misha hanson
captain

 Owner of the *Lightspinner*.

 When her rich father died, Misha could have lived in luxury – but that was much too boring.

 She spent all the money on the *Lightspinner* – and a life of adventure!

 Misha is the boss – but she doesn't always get her own way.

"Whenever we're in trouble, I know I've got a great team with me. The Starchasers will never let me down!"

suma

science officer

 He may look like a cat from Earth, but he is an alien with a brilliant mind for science – and sharp teeth and claws!

 Probably the smartest cat in space. Finn and Misha don't need to tell him that – he knows!

 Suma's not always easy to get on with. Take care – he makes a dangerous enemy!

"Misha tells people I'm just a big softy. The biggest softy in the galaxy. You know what? She's wrong."

finn
2021

pilot

- Finn is a great guy to have around when there's trouble – and for the Starchasers, that's most of the time.

- Probably the best pilot Planet Earth has ever produced – though Misha and Suma don't tell him that, of course!

- Finn is great for getting the Starchasers out of (and sometimes in to) trouble! If only he didn't love gadgets so much …

"I was in big trouble when Misha found me in an on-line computer game. She changed my life!"

model
Scout ship Model Q 590:
Lightspinner

date built
July, 2357

crew
Three

top speed
150 x light speed

acceleration
0 – light speed in
15.5 seconds

power
Faster than light – 2 Quantum Engines
Sub light speed – 2 Fermium Thrusters

landing craft
1 x Model LC250 Lander

communication
Spacenet™ multiphase

navigation system
R.O.B 57 series computer

*"THE TOP-OF-THE-RANGE SOUND
SYSTEM WILL BLOW YOUR MIND!"*
SPACE SOUNDS   APRIL 2357

"THE NEW Q590 – LIGHT SPEED IN 15.5 SECONDS – YOU'RE GONNA LOVE THIS BABY!"
WHAT SPACESHIP   JANUARY 2257

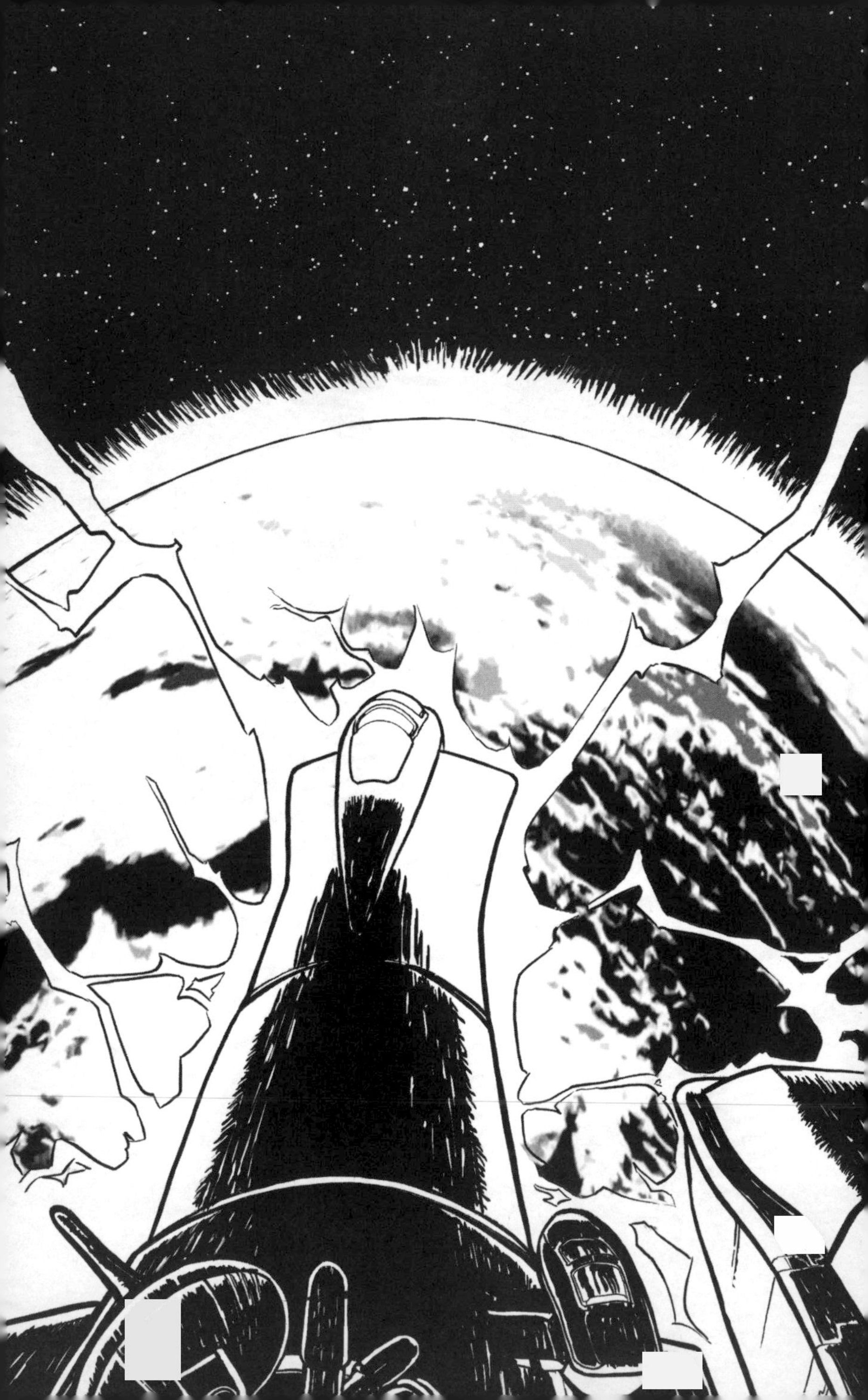

'WE'LL NEVER find them!'

'We'll never find them down there!'

Finn piloted the Lightspinner through the planet's atmosphere. The Starchasers were used to weird planets, but this one was – well, *weird*.

The Spacenet message had come through three days earlier. A ship called the Red Star had been sent to explore a new planet. There were six people on board.

The crew had sent a message when they reached the planet, but then the messages had suddenly stopped. The Lightspinner was only thirty light-years away. Could the Starchasers go and see what had happened?

It was a well-paid job, because it might be dangerous. But that was just the sort of job the Starchasers could do better than anyone else!

'The ship was working for a company back on Earth called Spacelife. They were looking for interesting alien plants,' Misha said.

'Why do they want plants?' asked Finn. 'There are loads of plants on Earth – I know, I live there!'

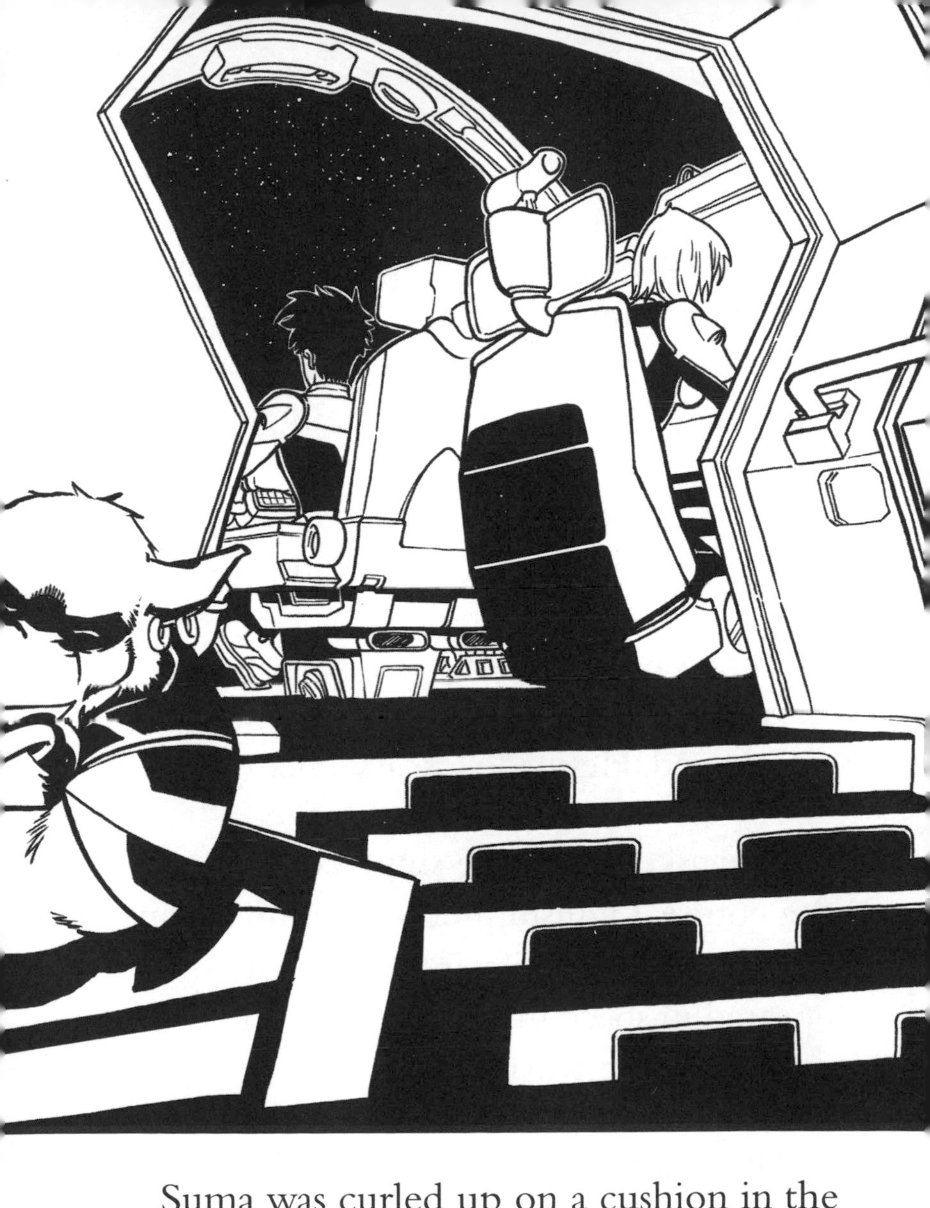

Suma was curled up on a cushion in the corner. Anyone looking at him would think he was asleep, but this was just what he did whenever he wasn't doing anything else. He flashed his big yellow eyes at Finn.

'They want plants for all sorts of reasons, you dumb human!' he said. 'New types of food, new types of medicine – maybe even something to improve your brain power!'

Suma was always rude to everyone, and no one took any notice. It was just his way.

Suma yawned, showing a mouthful of wickedly sharp teeth. It was just as well he was a friend. He made a scary enemy.

Finn asked Rob, the ship's computer, to set a course. Lightspinner's quantum engine began to hum, and a rainbow-coloured ring appeared in space in front of them. The entrance to the wormhole!

The engines hit full power and the Lightspinner vanished.

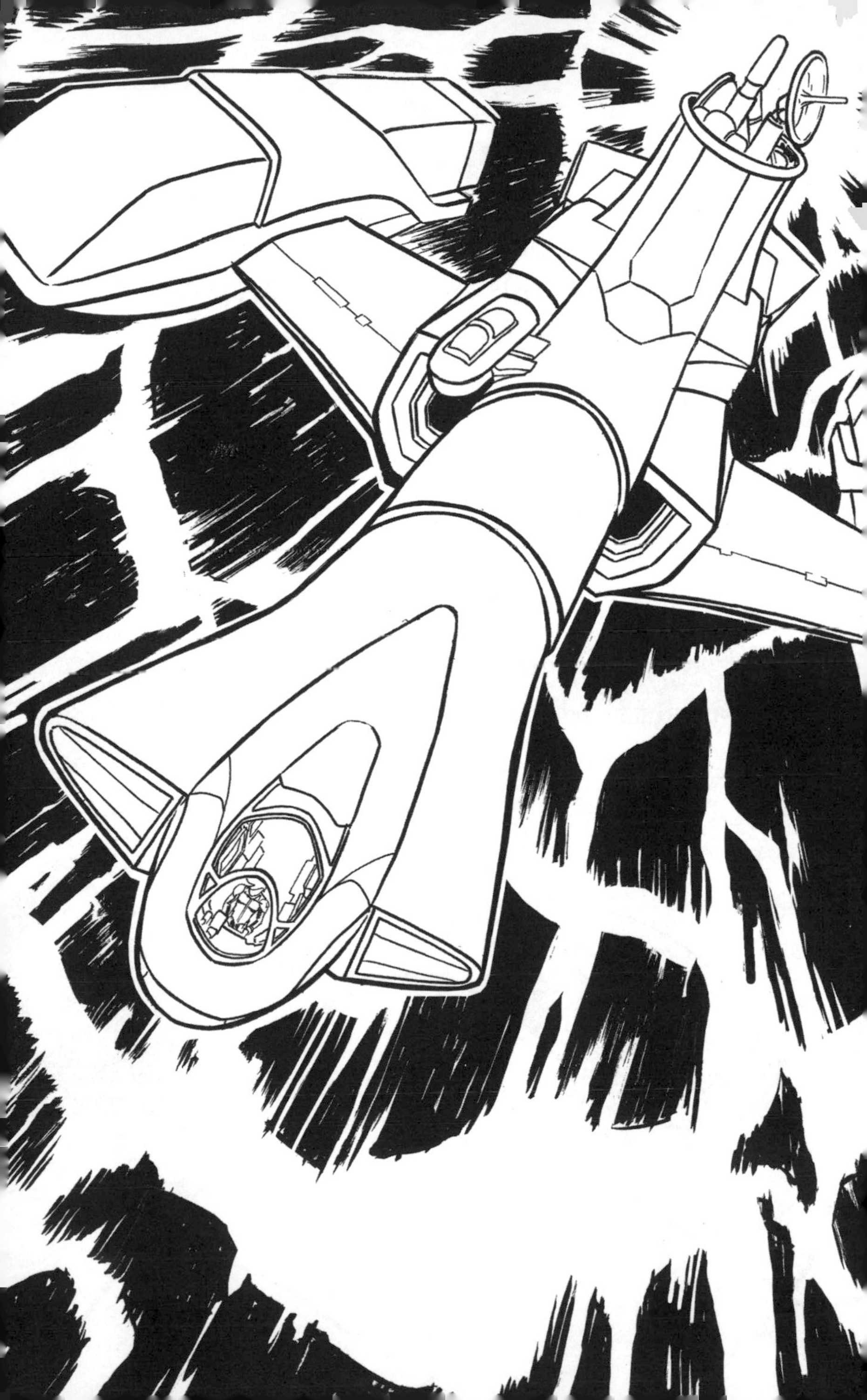

Now, three days later, the crew looked down on the surface of the planet.

'You know what?' said Finn. 'If it's plants they wanted, I reckon they came to the right place!'

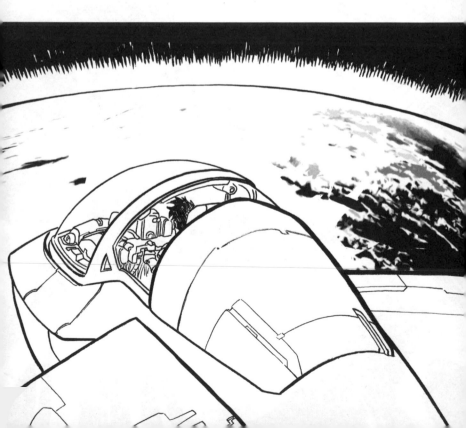

suma twitches his whiskers

Most planets had a bit of everything –
forests, deserts, cold, icy bits, blazing hot bits,
mountains, valleys. This planet had just one
thing. Plants.

Wherever they looked, there was a carpet
of green. It stretched right round the planet.
It grew higher around the equator where
the sun was hot, but even the cold north
and south poles were covered.

Suma checked the air. They could breathe it, so they wouldn't need space suits.

'What do we do now?' asked Finn.

'I'm sending out a radio message in case they can hear us. If their distress beacon is working, we should be able to hear it if we get anywhere near it. We've got to fly over as much of the planet as we can and just wait. It's all we can do.'

Suma jumped down from his cushion and stared at the view screen. His whiskers twitched.

'Not quite all. I want some of that plant. Captain, I'm heading down in the lander. O.K.?'

Misha knew that Suma was deadly serious whenever he twitched his whiskers. She never argued.

'O.K., Suma. You and Finn go. I'll stay with the ship.'

Finn never argued with Suma either. Mainly because he always lost.

the surface
-or is it?

'But Suma, how are we going to land?
There's no bare ground anywhere!'

'Just keep going down. If we can't land,
I'll grab some of the plant when we get
near.'

Finn thought Suma was crazy. But then
again, Finn often thought that, and he was

usually wrong.

They got closer and closer to the surface. At last, they were almost touching the plant.

'It's like a thick green mat!' said Finn. 'I wonder if we could land on it?'

'We could give it a try,' said Suma.

Slowly, slowly the lander settled down on to the green mat of plants. Suma kept quiet. He knew that Finn was one of the best pilots around. If anyone could land here, he could.

'O.K. Cutting engines.'

'Brilliant, Finn. Stay with the lander. I'll just get a piece of the plant and I'll be right back.'

Suma leapt down. A short distance away, a piece of plant with white flowers and seed pods stuck up into the air.

Suma walked on the knuckles of his hands. His long fingers – not like any Earth cat – were curled up into a fist. When he reached the flowers he stretched out his front paw to snap off the branch. He was just putting it into his back-pack when he heard Finn shouting.

'Suma, get over here, quick! I'm sinking!'

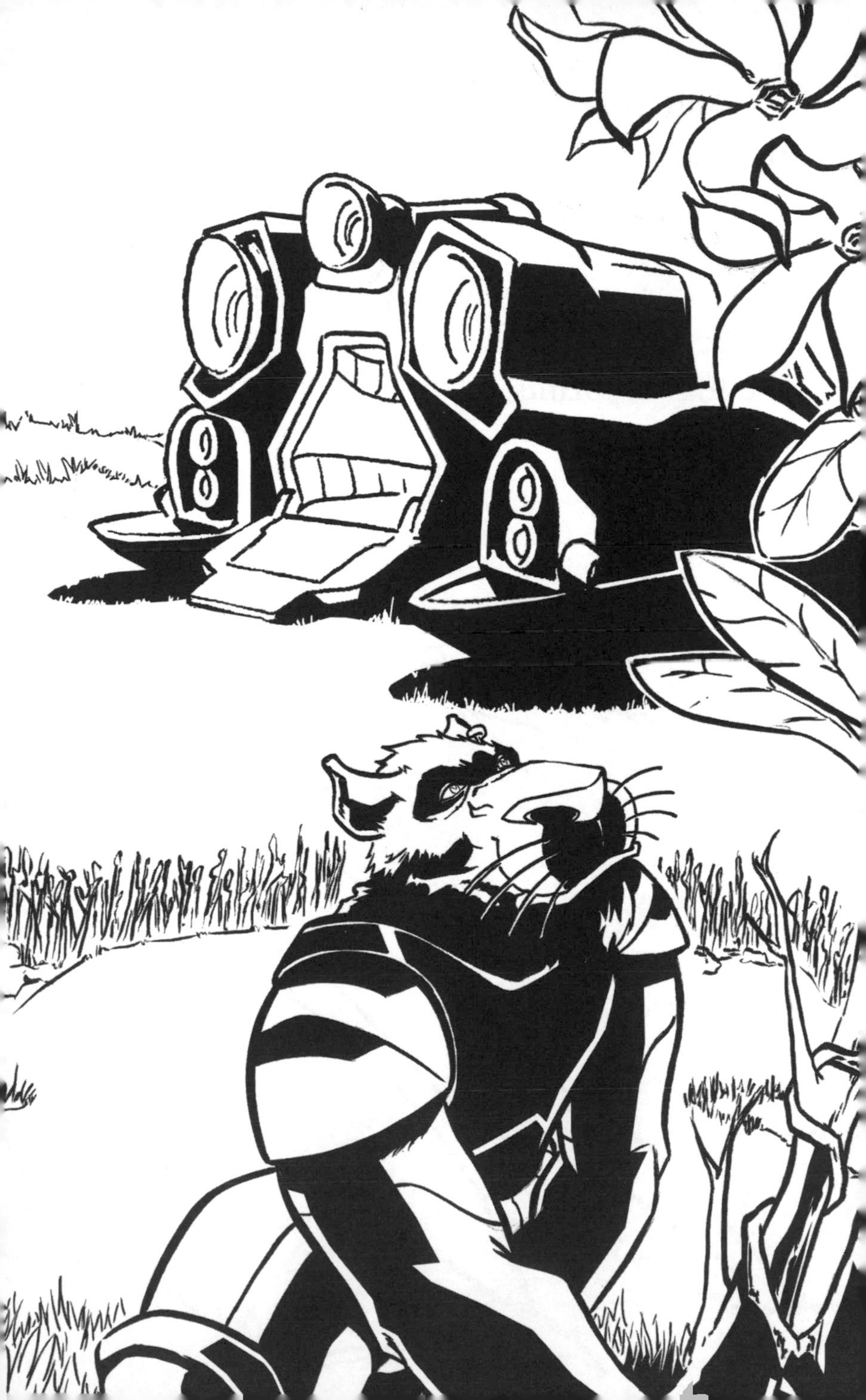

With four legs, Suma could run faster than any man. In seconds he was back at the lander. He saw why Finn had shouted.

Water was bubbling up around the legs of the lander, which was sinking deeper into the mass of plants!

Suma leapt into the open door.

'Up! Quick!'

The plants had somehow become tangled round the bottom of the lander, and Finn needed full power to break free.

'Phew! That was close!'

But Suma wasn't listening. He was busy looking at the broken-off piece of plant.

'Now I know why it's so difficult to land,' he said.

'Why?'

'There isn't any land.'

ocean
planet

Back on the Lightspinner, the Starchasers were having a meeting.

'This planet is one big ocean,' Suma told them. 'The plants are like a great mat floating on it. Luckily the lander is very light, or it would have broken through and sunk to the bottom. That's what probably happened to the Red Star. Like us, they thought they could land on the plants. Before they knew what was happening, the ship sank through

into the sea. This is really fast-growing stuff. The hole they made will have filled up by now.'

'Not much chance of finding them alive then,' said Finn gloomily. 'And no rescue, no money.'

'I'm not giving up that easily,' said Misha. 'Spaceships can survive in really deep water. After all, they have to survive in space!'

'You think they might still be alive?'

'Could be. We'll just have to keep looking. Their distress beacon will work under water. We'll have to get a bit lower though, if we're going to pick up anything.'

The Starchasers carried on with the search. Piloting the ship was tough. Spaceships aren't designed to fly well in an atmosphere, especially near the ground where it is hard to know what the wind is going to do next. But Misha knew that Finn was up for it.

'Hey, look! Smoke! Could that be them?'

'Let's check it out.'

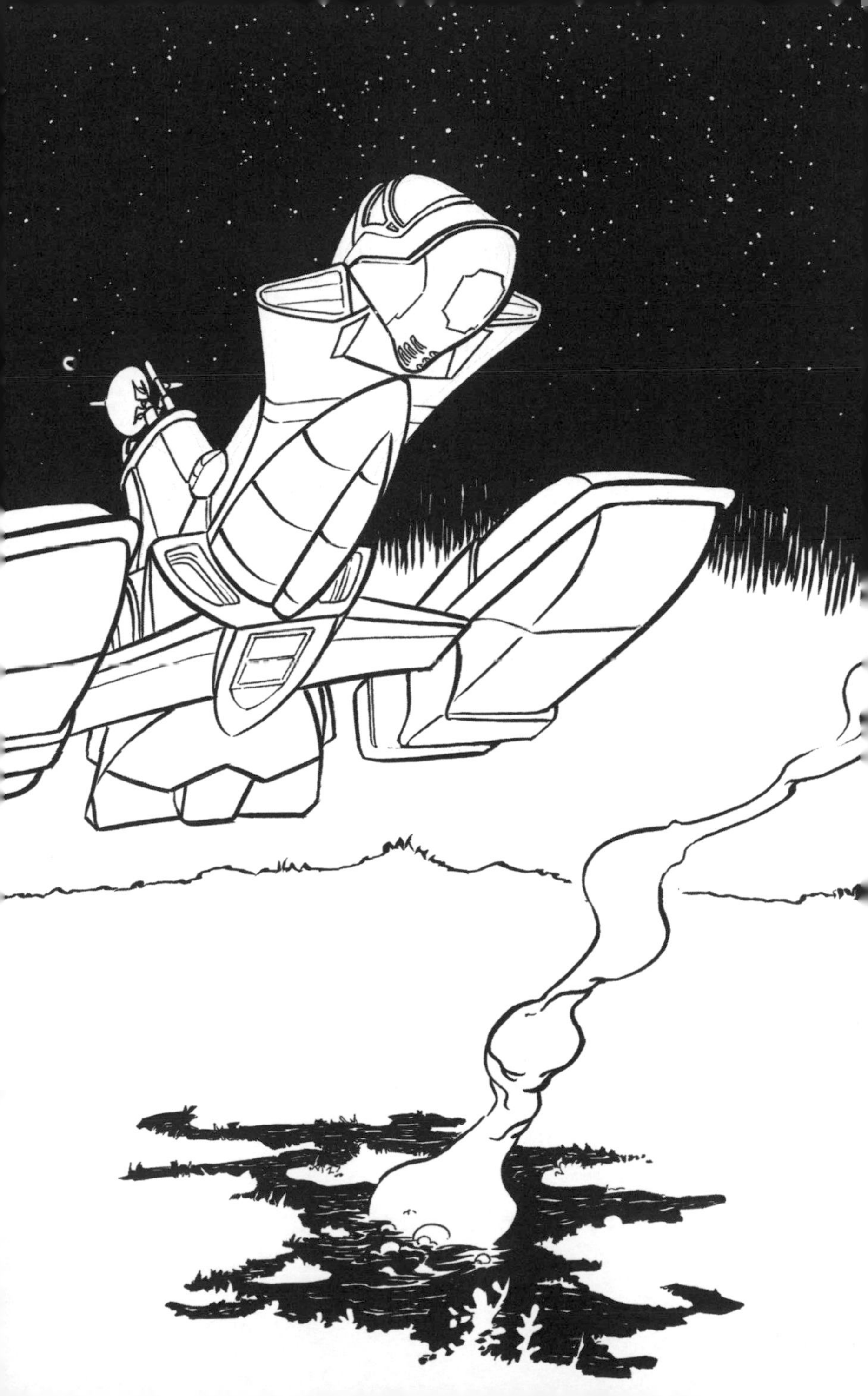

Finn flew closer. Below was a circle of water, the only time they'd seen the surface of the sea. The plants round the edge seemed to be shrivelled and brown.

'Look at those bubbles! That water's hot!'

'What's going on?'

Suma knew.

'Underwater volcano. That's why the water on this planet doesn't freeze, even at the poles. The volcanoes warm it up, and the plants trap the heat.'

The Starchasers carried on searching. Misha was worried. Flying this low was hard on Finn. Another couple of days and they would have to give up. She hated giving up, especially when she thought about six people trapped in their spaceship at the bottom of the ocean.

Then they heard something.

the beacon

It was faint at first, but as they moved to where the sound was coming from, it got louder. The distress beacon!

Finn hovered over the spot where the sound was loudest.

'Looks like we've found them.'

'Now all we've got to do is get them up. Any ideas?'

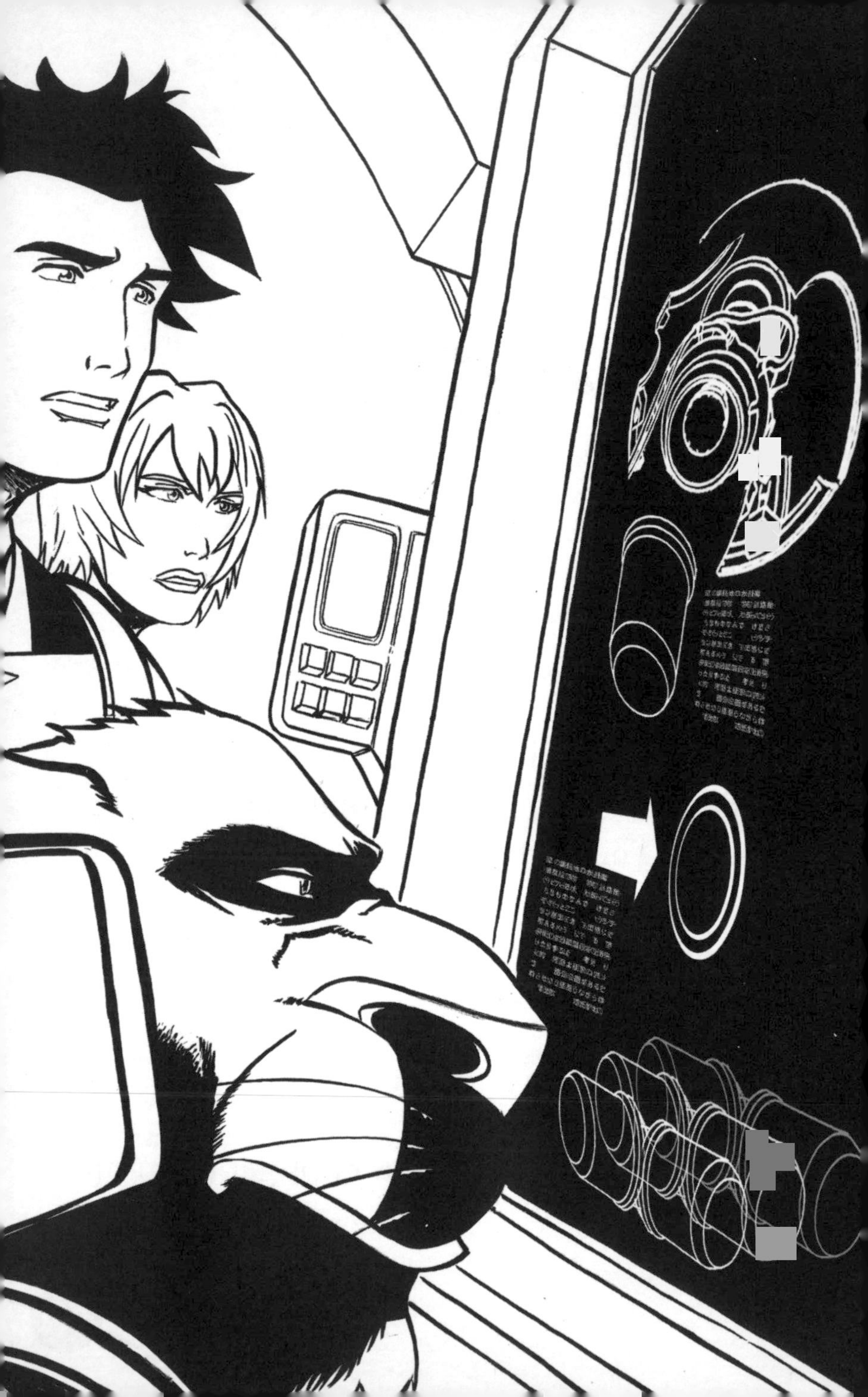

'We need a base down there,' said Suma. 'It shouldn't be difficult. I can walk around on the plants fine, and if we put floats on the lander it won't sink.'

'That still doesn't get the guys on the bottom of sea out of there,' said Finn. 'And we don't know how deep the ship is. We don't even know if they're still alive.'

'One thing at a time!' said Misha. 'If you and Suma can set up the base, I can take the Lightspinner back into space and switch off the engines. We can keep in touch by radio.'

'That's good, said Suma. 'But I'm going to need some stuff to take with us. Give me an hour or two.'

Two hours later, Suma and Finn were heading back down to the planet's surface.

The lander was fitted with wide floats so it wouldn't sink.

Once on the surface, they started setting up the base. The two Starchasers bolted some metal sheets together to make a surface they could walk on easily.

Suma first wanted to work out how deep the sea was. He had brought a piece of kit to do that.

'It's called an echo sounder,' said Suma. 'It was invented centuries ago, but still works well.'

He checked the readings. 'That's good. The sea is quite shallow here. Now to try and get in touch with the Red Star.'

But then the plants began to move.

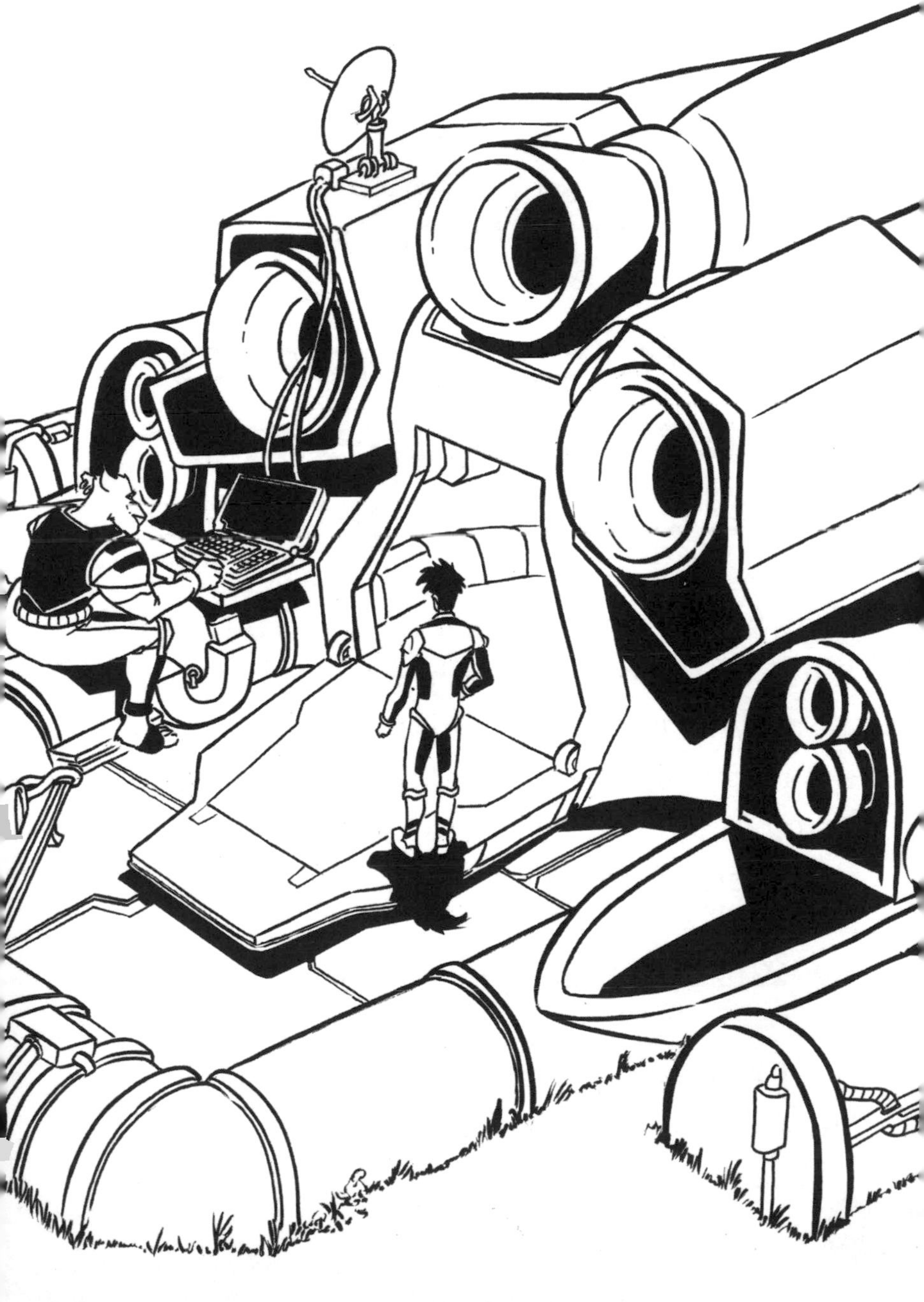

UOLCANOES
-and giant
KILLEr fish

First, a great circle of plants just a couple of hundred metres away seemed to lift in the air and fall back again. Ripples spread out, the mat bouncing up and down. It was like being in a boat in a storm. At last, everything settled down again.

'What was that?' yelled Finn.

'I think a volcano is erupting. Hope the lander's O.K.'

Finn checked it out and it seemed fine. But Suma was worried.

'That was only a small one. If a big eruption's coming, it's not going to be safe around here. Let's see if we can contact the Red Star.'

Suma pushed a metal rod down through the plants. It was a radio aerial.

'Hello, Red Star. Lightspinner here. What is your situation?'

The reply came almost straight away.

'Hello, Lightspinner. Are we pleased to hear you! We tried to land on the surface and ended up down here! We've got serious damage to the outside of the ship so we can't move. And something happened just now – we got shook up really badly! What was all that about? And how are you going to get us out of here?'

'It was a volcano erupting. Not sure we can do much for your ship. But your space-suits should be fine underwater. We can lower a chain and pull you up.'

'Good idea – but there's a problem. We'll be eaten before we get up there. There are giant killer fish!'

'how do we get them out?'

'Giant *what*?'

'Killer fish. We lost Abe that way. He went out in his suit to try and fix the ship. This great fish came along and got him. It was horrible!'

'O.K., don't worry. We'll think of something. I'll get back to you.'

They thought about it, then thought some more, but not even Suma had a brilliant idea.

'Hey, can you smell that?' said Suma suddenly.

'Smell what?'

'You humans are useless! No sense of smell at all! I know what it is now! It's gas bubbling up from the volcano! We'd better get our suits on – this stuff is pretty poisonous!'

Finn and Suma climbed into their space-suits. The suits could protect them against poison gas, or the cold of outer space, but they weren't much use against killer fish.

'Hang on, I've thought of something!'

Suma went into the lander and brought out another piece of kit. He stuck it down through the plant.

'Quiet now.'

Suma listened carefully through head-phones. Then he went back to the radio and called the Red Star.

'Hi guys. We're in luck. The volcano near your ship is about to blow, and it's pouring hot poisonous gases into the sea.'

'You call that luck?'

'I've just checked on the sound scan. I can hear those giant killer fish of yours – and they're swimming away as fast as they can. They must know what's coming! It'll be quite safe to leave the ship!'

The crew of the Red Star weren't convinced. They didn't want to end up getting eaten, like poor Abe.

'How can you be so sure?'

'I'm absolutely sure! And just to prove it, I'm going to send Finn here down to you with the chain!'

why does it have to be me?'

'Why does it have to be me?'

'Cos I'm the brains, and you're the muscle. Anyway, you keep calling me a cat. Cats hate swimming.'

At last, Finn agreed. He had trusted Suma with his life many times, and he'd never been let down.

Finn got out a laser torch and burnt a hole through the plant. It was about two metres thick. He took the end of the chain and dropped it into the hole.

Finn had fitted weights on his suit – the ones they used on low gravity planets. They would help him sink quickly into the water.

No sunlight reached down through the plants, and at first everything was totally dark. But as he floated down Finn saw a red glow beneath him. It was lava, gushing out from the undersea volcano! He checked the temperature of the water. Getting hot. Luckily his suit was able to keep the heat out.

Clang! His feet hit the metal hull of the Red Star. Right on target! But the lava was not far away, and was creeping nearer.

With a shock, Finn realised he had been so busy watching the lava he had forgotten about the killer fish. Just as well – it wasn't a happy thought.

The ship's airlock was open. Finn went inside and shut the outer door. The inner

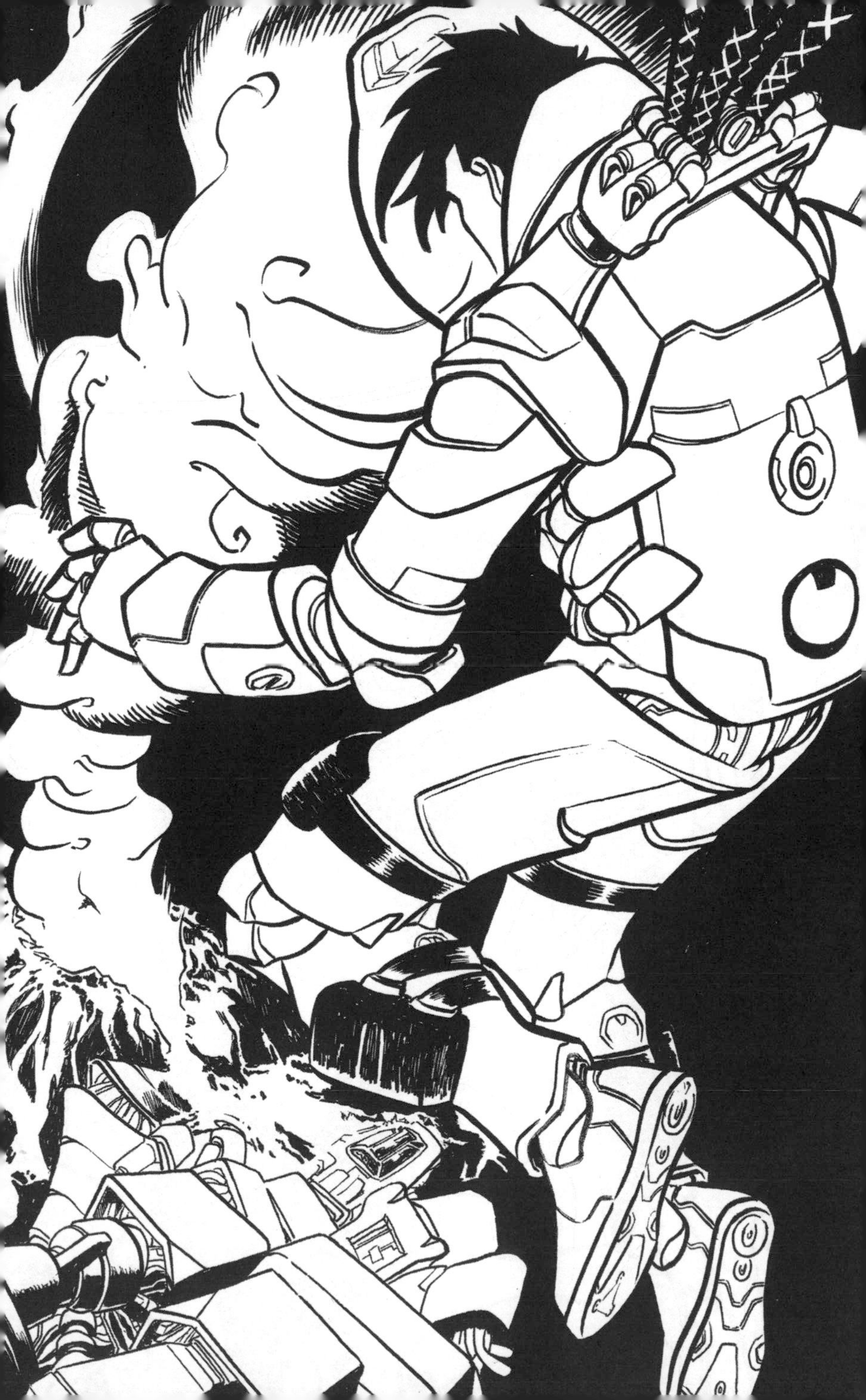

door opened. Were the crew of the Red Star pleased to see him!

Finn didn't waste time on hellos.

'Grab anything important you can carry and let's go. That lava is getting nearer, and

the volcano could blow at any minute.'

Suma had fixed a winch on to the chain. He hauled Finn and the Red Star crew up two at a time.

'Quick, guys, into the lander.'

It was a squash but they all made it in. When they were a mile or so up in the air, they looked down. The piece of plant they had been sitting on wasn't there any more – there was just a big round hole where the water seethed and bubbled.

A week later the crew of the Lightspinner were back at their base on Earth. Finn and Misha were relaxing, but Suma was nowhere to be seen.

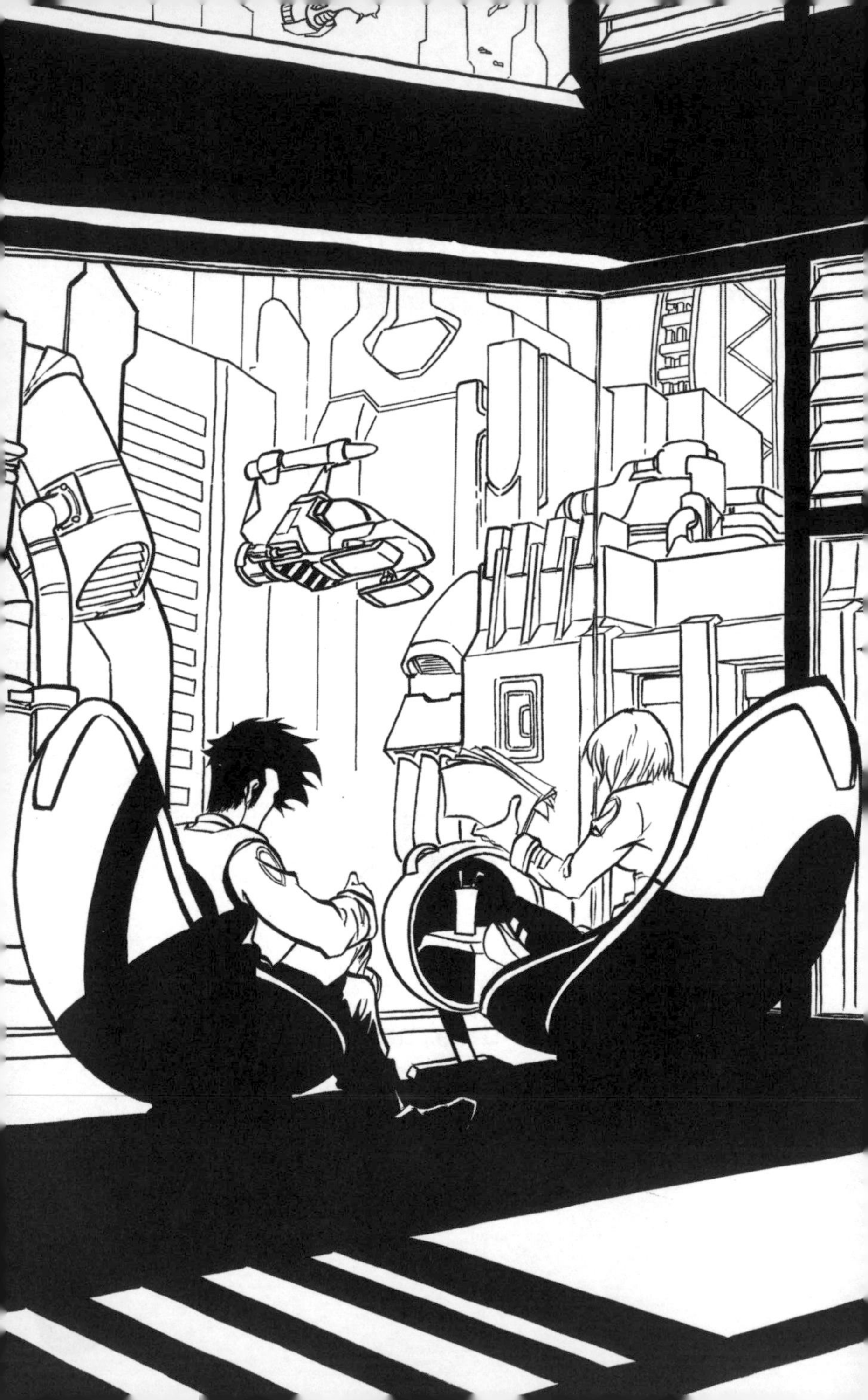

'He's in his lab. Says he's doing some tests.'

At last Suma arrived. He was carrying a tray of nuts. He pushed it at Finn.

'You like nuts. Try one of these.'

Finn popped two or three into his mouth.

'Suma, these are delicious! Where did you get them?'

'They're the seeds of that plant on the ocean world. And as we're the first people to find them, I think we can set up a good little business selling them!'

'But Suma, how do you know they're not poisonous?'

'I don't. That's why I gave some to you to try. Feeling O.K., are you?'

That was the trouble with Suma. You never knew if he was joking.